P9-DDB-092

Hello, Harvest Moon

by Ralph Fletcher

illustrated by Kate Kiesler

Clarion Books
New York

Clarion Books
a Houghton Mifflin Company imprint
215 Park Avenue South, New York, NY 10003
Text copyright © 2003 by Ralph Fletcher
Illustrations copyright © 2003 by Kate Kiesler

The illustrations were executed in oil paint.
The text was set in 21-point Bernhard Modern Bold.

Printed in Singapore.

www.houghtonmifflinbooks.com

Library of Congress Cataloging-in-Publication Data

Fletcher, Ralph J.
Hello, harvest moon / by Ralph Fletcher ; illustrated by Kate Kiesler.
p. cm.
Summary: Poetic prose describes a full autumn moon and the magical effect
it has on the earth, plants, animals, and people around it.
ISBN 0-618-16451-0 (alk. paper)
[1. Moon—Fiction. 2. Nature—Fiction.] I. Kiesler, Kate, ill. II. Title.
PZ7.F632115 He 2003
[E]—dc21   2002015541

TWP 10 9 8 7 6 5 4 3 2 1

For my sisters—
Elaine, Kathy, Carolyn—
who heard Mom sing
the moon song
when they were little girls
—R.F.

In memory of Jasper, who came
and left near the harvest moon
—K.K.

The crops have been gathered.
The pumpkins have been picked.
The silos are filled to bursting
with a million ears of corn.
Tired farmers are fast asleep.

But something is stirring
at the edge of the world.
Something is rising
low in the trees.

It comes up round, ripe, and huge
over autumn fields of corn and wheat.
Hello, harvest moon.

With silent slippers
it climbs the night stairs,
lifting free of the treetops
to start working its magic,
staining earth and sky with a ghostly glow.

8

Harvest moonlight brushes your face,
makes you stir and blink, wake and wonder,
"Who left that outside light on?"

What radiance is streaming into your room!
It's so bright, you can read your favorite book
without even turning on the lamp.

9

Outside, the yards and streets seem to be
covered by a sparkling tablecloth.
Birch trees shine as if they have been
double-dipped
                in moonlight.

If you're lucky, you might spy
a few large luna moths
performing their ballet
in the crisp, cool air.

A garden spider builds her web,
hoping to catch an insect
drawn to the great lamp
in the sky.

Milkweed pods have cracked open,
spilling out spores
like tiny moonlings
                    floating
                            up to their mother.

15

If you played a nocturnal game of hide-and-go-seek
and hid behind that huge pine tree,
you would be almost invisible,
cloaked in moonshadow.

15

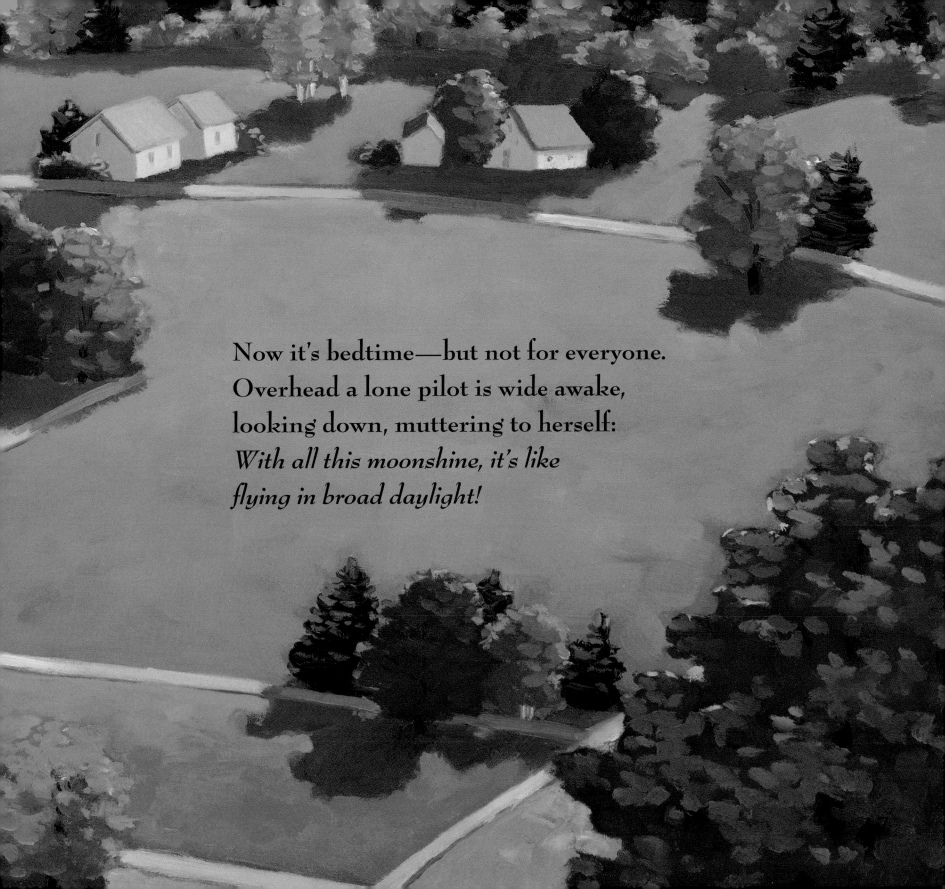

Now it's bedtime—but not for everyone.
Overhead a lone pilot is wide awake,
looking down, muttering to herself:
*With all this moonshine, it's like
flying in broad daylight!*

A night watchman gets out of his bed,
pulling on his boots, filling his thermos.
He always packs his flashlight,
though he wonders if he'll need it,
going to work on a night like this.

19

The harvest moon has its own work to do.
It paints the wings of owls and nighthawks
with a mixture of silver and shadow.

It speaks to the moonflower—
Now! Now!
and sweet white blossoms unfold,
though only night creatures
will see them.

It whispers to geese,
Away! Away!
and they become restless
to start the long flight south.

23

Baby turtles emerge from eggs
tucked beneath the blanket of sand
where their mother left them
two months ago.
They make a mad dash to the ocean.

24

The harvest moon moves the earth's waters.
Grabbing whole oceans with its arms,
it pulls in the high tide
that will lift all the boats,
        every rowboat and yacht,
                tied snug at the dock.

It floods the clam flats with lonely lunar light,
setting off an eruption of bubbles
from clams and crabs
tucked in mud.

28

It floods us with dreams and memories
of every full moon we have ever seen.
It connects us to our distant ancestors
who prayed to the harvest moon,
yet feared it might be a god's
one unblinking eye.

Finally, it starts to ease lower . . .

. . . sprinkling silver coins
like a careless millionaire
over ponds, lakes, and seas,
till all the money is spent.

When you wake up,
look to the western horizon
and you might catch the moonset:
a sleepy head
        winking
            falling
                slow motion
                    onto its pillow.

Good night, harvest moon.

32